THE EVERYDAY ADVENTURES OF

PAPA & PAWS™

THE TWINS TAKE OVER!

WORDS & PICTURES
BY PAPA PAWS

For our beloved Zoe, our fuzzy little angel, furever in our hearts.

For Marley, our sweet and fuzzy puppy, who fills our days with joy.

Sign up for our email newsletter at www.papaandpaws.com for cute and fuzzy updates, *plus* get a free short story eBook!

ISBN 978-1-7345998-3-1

First edition published January 5, 2021

A HAPPYLAND PRESS BOOK

Our Grand Dame, Miss Mia of Yorkshire.

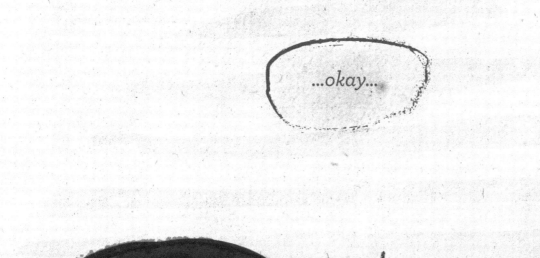

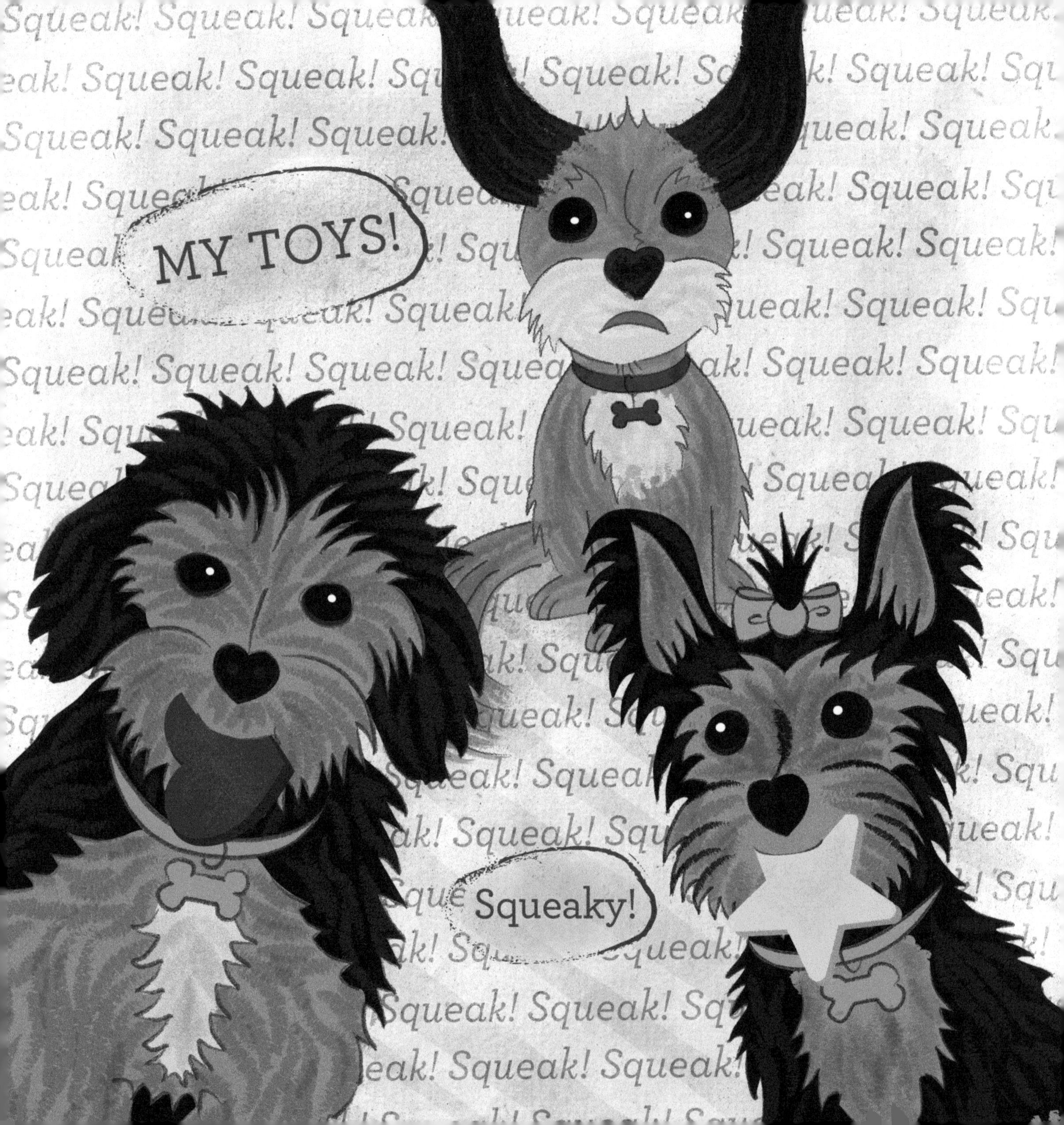
MY TOYS!
Squeaky!

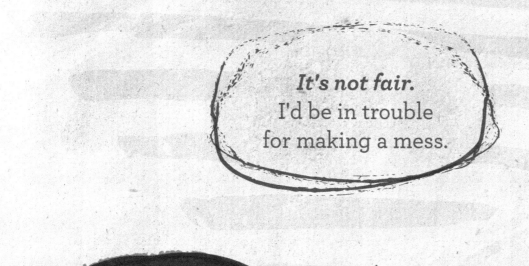

Being a *big sister*
is hard.

This *whole yard* is ours. We can *run and play* out here.
Neato!
So cool!

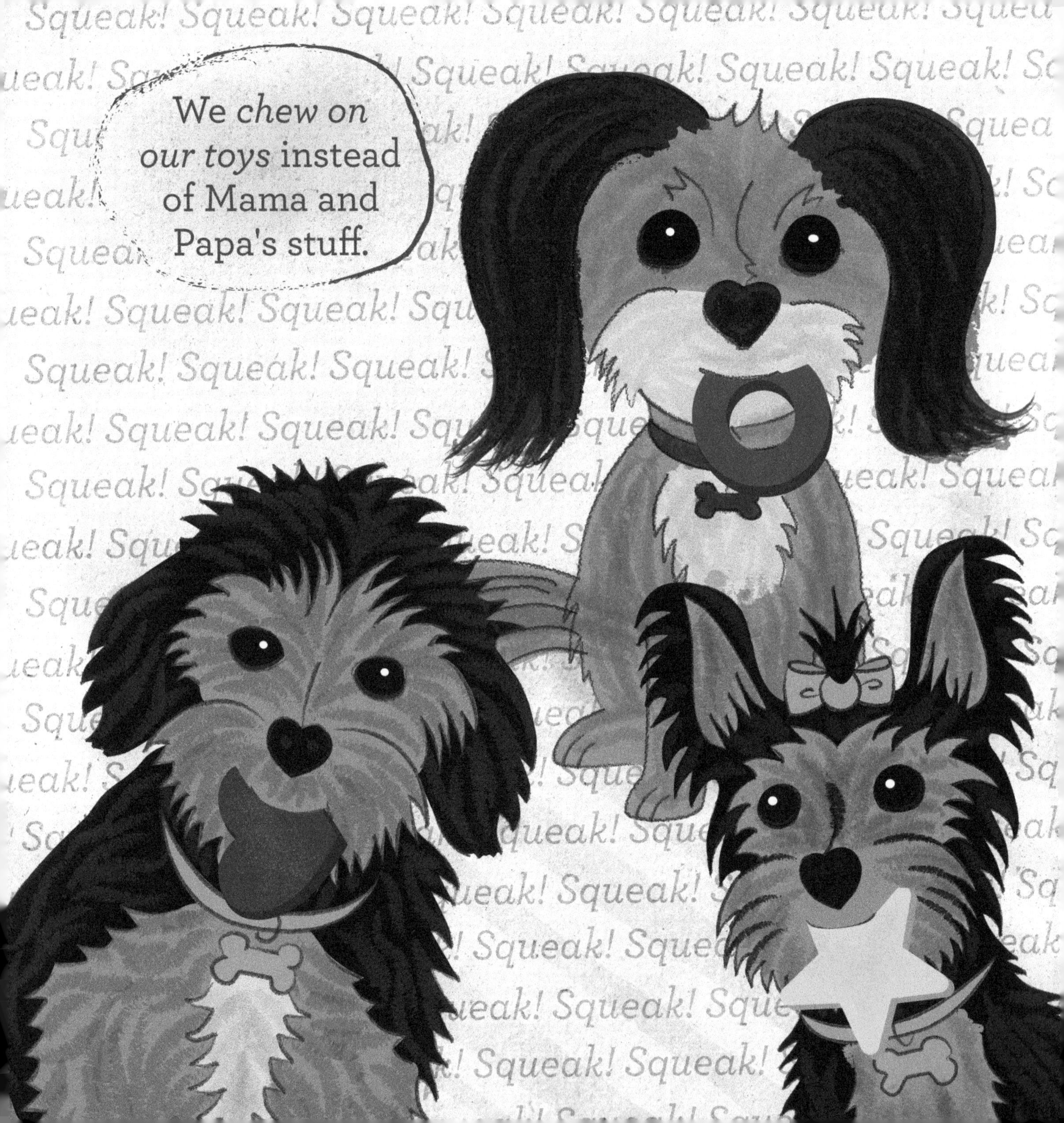
We *chew on our toys* instead of Mama and Papa's stuff.

ZzzZzzZzz

ZzzZzzZzz

This is how we nap.

CPSIA information can be obtained
at www.ICGtesting.com
Printed in the USA
LVHW072128291220
675305LV00017B/449